P9-CEF-720

HELLO KITTY®

What Will You Be A to Z?

Abrams Books for Young Readers, New York

Tippy's Takeout

Certificate

Mrs. Sweet's Shoppe

One sunny day, Hello Kitty was skipping home from town.

Thinking of all the nice people she had met and of the many fun things that they do,

she began to wonder what she would be when she grew up. Starting with A and

ending with Z, she imagined all sorts of possibilities!

Hello A! Hello Artist!

Aa Bb Cc Dd Ee Ff Gg Hh Ii Jj

alphabet

Kk Ll Mm Nn Oo

Pp Qq Rr Ss Tt Uu

arrow

Vv Ww Xx Yy Zz

acorn

airplane

apple

apron

ape

accordion

aquarium

As an artist, Hello Kitty would paint bright and colorful pictures in her studio.

Hello B! Hello Ballerina!

butterfly

bee

bird

berries

basket

bouquet

bear

As a ballerina, Hello Kitty would pirouette across the stage in a cute pink tutu.

Hello C! Hello Cowgirl!

cloud

cow

cactus

corn

caterpillar

cotton

chicken

campfire

As a cowgirl, Hello Kitty would ride her horse into the sunset!

Hello D! Hello Doctor!

doll

daisies

Dear Daniel

Doctor of Medicine Degree
hereby presented with honors to
Hello Kitty

diploma

dish

desk

door

dog

duck

As a doctor, Hello Kitty would help those who are sick.

Hello E! Hello Explorer!

east

elephant

envelope

eagle

earthworm

elk

eggs

eggplant

As an explorer, Hello Kitty would travel to exotic places and see strange and unusual things.

Hello F! Hello Fashion Designer!

feathers

flowers

fan

Fifi

fabric

fez

frog

flamingo

As a fashion designer, Hello Kitty would create dresses with hats to match.

Hello G! Hello Gardener!

giraffe · Grandma · geraniums · grapes · Grandpa · gourds · goose · grasshopper · goat

As a gardener, Hello Kitty would grow pretty flowers, delicious fruits, and lots of vegetables.

Hello H! Hello Hairdresser!

heart

hello

hamburger

hat

hanger

honey

honey

hairbrush

hair spray

extra hold

handbag

As a hairdresser, Hello Kitty would style her friends' hair.

Hello I! Hello Ice-Skater!

icicles

ice skates

igloo

irises

ice cream

As an ice-skater, Hello Kitty would swirl and glide across the glistening ice.

Hello J! Hello Juggler!

juggle

jam jars

Joey

jump

Jodie

As a juggler, Hello Kitty would juggle bowling pins and more!

Hello K! Hello Kindergarten Teacher!

kite

kangaroo

keys

knit cap

knapsack

As a kindergarten teacher, Hello Kitty would teach her students their ABCs!

Hello L! Hello Librarian!

light

lamp

ladder

lollipop

leaf

lion

letter

Dear Hello Kitty,
Thank you for
finding the book
I wanted.
Sincerely,
Thomas

ladybug

lemonade

As a librarian, Hello Kitty would help people find the books that they need.

Hello M! Hello Movie Star!

moon

mask

HOLLYWOOD

Mory

Mama

motorcar

Mimmy

makeup

magazine

medal

mirror

messenger

mail

As a movie star, Hello Kitty would impress audiences everywhere with her charm and talent.

Hello N! Hello Newspaper Reporter!

newspapers

NATURE

net

nest

newt

nautilus

noon

NEIGHBORS

newlyweds

necklace   necktie

narcissus

noodles

notepad

NATIONAL

nurse

napkin

As a newspaper reporter, Hello Kitty would write stories about many interesting things.

Hello O! Hello Opera Singer!

owl

ostrich

orchids

ovation

orchestra

oboe

As an opera singer, Hello Kitty would wear an opulent gown during her performance.

Hello P! Hello Pastry Chef!

peach

plum

petit four

peppermint sticks

pear

pineapple

pie

pastry platter

pancakes

pumpkin

pretzel

puff pastry

present

As a pastry chef, Hello Kitty would bake delicious desserts and yummy treats.

Hello Q! Hello Queen!

quarter horses

quill

The Queen's Notes

quartet

quail

As a queen, Hello Kitty would wear a crown covered with sparkling jewels.

Hello R! Hello Race Car Driver!

rocket

race cars

racetrack

Rorry

roses

roller skates

As a race car driver, Hello Kitty would win the Indy 500!

Hello S! Hello Scientist!

star

satellite

spatula

scissors

spider

sink

soap

sunflower

shells

snail

sneakers

scale

As a scientist, Hello Kitty would look through a microscope and see many fascinating things.

Hello T! Hello Tour Guide!

towers

trees

train

tiger

Tippy

Thomas

taxicab

Tracy

Tim & Tammy

tricycle

As a tour guide, Hello Kitty would take her friends to see wonderful sights in faraway places!

Hello U! Hello Undercover Agent!

unicorn

ultraviolet sunglasses

uniform

umbrella

underground tunnel

As an undercover agent, Hello Kitty would decode secret messages!

Hello V! Hello Violinist!

velvet curtain

vine

violin

violets

vase

votives

vocalist

valentine

be mine

As a violinist, Hello Kitty would play grand symphonies in the string section of an orchestra.

Hello W! Hello Writer!

Once upon a time there was a beautiful and very intelligent young girl who had magical powers. One day while she was watering her flowers, she looked at her watch, which said it was noon. She saw a worm wiggling in the dirt and right near it was something shiny that caught her eye. It was a wedding ring!

watering can

wedding ring

worm

watch

As a writer, Hello Kitty would tell the tale of the great adventures of a daring heroine!

Hello X! Hello Xylophonist!

xylophone

As a xylophonist, Hello Kitty would play beautiful music for her friends.

Hello Y! Hello Yoga Master!

yellow snapper

yacht

yoga

yellow jasmine

yellow-bellied sapsucker

As a yoga master, Hello Kitty would teach peace and tranquility through yoga!

Hello Z! Hello Zoologist!

zebra butterfly

zebra finch

zebu

zebras

zebra fish

As a zoologist, Hello Kitty would study all her favorite animals, large and small.

It's the end of the day and of the ABCs, but

Hello Kitty has only just begun to imagine all the fun things that she might be

when she grows up. And now that you know the alphabet, too . . .

. . . what do YOU want to be, A to Z?

The Library of Congress has cataloged the 2003 edition of this book as follows:

Library of Congress Cataloging-in-Publication Data
Glaser, Higashi.
Hello Kitty what will I be A to Z? / illustrated by Higashi Glaser.
p. cm.
Summary: Hello Kitty thinks of different occupations, from artist to
zoologist, that she might like to be when she grows up.
ISBN 0-8109-4595-9
[1. Cats—Fiction. 2. Occupations—Fiction. 3. Alphabet.] I. Title.
PZ7.G48046Hdk 2003
[E]—dc21
2003003833

ISBN for the 2013 edition: 978-1-4197-0911-1

Hello Kitty® characters, names, and all related indicia are trademarks of SANRIO CO., LTD.
Used Under License. Copyright © 1976, 2003, 2013 SANRIO CO., LTD.

Text and original art copyright © 2003, 2013 SANRIO CO., LTD.

This edition published in 2013 by Abrams Books for Young Readers, an imprint of ABRAMS. All rights reserved. No
portion of this book may be reproduced, stored in a retrieval system, or transmitted in any form or by any means,
mechanical, electronic, photocopying, recording, or otherwise, without written permission from the publisher.

Printed and bound in China
10 9 8 7 6 5 4 3 2 1

Abrams Books for Young Readers are available at special discounts when purchased in quantity for premiums and
promotions as well as fundraising or educational use. Special editions can also be created to specification. For details,
contact specialsales@abramsbooks.com or the address below.

ABRAMS
THE ART OF BOOKS SINCE 1949
115 West 18th Street
New York, NY 10011
www.abramsbooks.com

Hello Kitty's

ABC Stencil Fun

Aa Bb Cc

Gg Hh Ii

Mm Nn

Qq Rr Ss

Ww Xx

To use your Hello Kitty alphabet stencil, carefully punch out each letter.

Dd Ee Ff
Ij Kk Ll
Oo Pp
Tt Uu Vv
y Zz

With a pencil, trace the letters to make the words you want to write.
Then color everything in with crayons, colored pencils, or Magic Markers!